P9-DVM-759

# My Name Is Aviva

For my grandmother,
Ruth Levin (1890–1989).
May her memory be a blessing
—L.N.

For Michal with love
—A.J.

KAR-BEN PUBLISHING
A division of Lerner Publishing Group, Inc.
241 First Avenue North
Minneapolis, MN 55401 USA
1-800-4-KARBEN

Website address: www.karben.com

Main body text set in Rough LT Com 17/21.
Typeface provided by Linotype AG.

Library of Congress Cataloging-in-Publication Data

Newman, Leslea.
    My name is Aviva / by Lesléa Newman ; illustrated by Ag Jatkowska.
        pages   cm.
    Summary: "Aviva isn't happy with her unusual name until she hears wonderful things about her great-grandmother, after whom she was named" — Provided by publisher.
    ISBN 978-1-4677-2654-2 (lib. bdg. : alk. paper)
    [1. Names, Personal—Fiction. 2. Great-grandmothers—Fiction. 3. Jews—United States—Fiction.] I.
Jatkowska, Ag, illustrator. II. Title.
PZ7.N47988My  2015
    [E]—dc23
2014003664

Manufactured in the United States of America
1 — CG — 12/31/14

# My Name Is Aviva

Lesléa Newman

Illustrated by
Ag Jatkowska

KAR-BEN
PUBLISHING

My name is Aviva, but the other kids never call me that.

"Bye, Amoeba!" Danny yells, as he runs past me in the schoolyard to meet his dad.

"My name is Aviva, not Amoeba!" I shout, but Danny just runs on.

Then Josette, who is French, skips by.
"Au revoir, Viva La France!" she calls.

"My name is not Viva La France! My name is Aviva," I scream, but Josette is already gone.

I climb the monkey bars and hang upside down ignoring everybody.

Finally Mommy and Lulu arrive. "Ready to go, Aviva?" Mommy asks.

I don't answer.

"Aviva?" Mommy taps my shoulder, and Lulu sniffs my knee.

I don't move.

"Aviva, let's go."

"My name isn't Aviva," I tell Mommy. "My name is Emily."

"Emily? I'm sorry. I thought you were my daughter. Come, Lulu, let's go find Aviva." Mommy turns away.

"Wait, Mommy." I jump off the swing. "I am your daughter. But I've changed my name to Emily."

"Well then let's go, Emily," Mommy says.

"Mommy," I say as we crunch through autumn leaves. "Can I ask you something?"

"You just did," Mommy answers. She always says that.

"Can I ask you something else?"

"You just did," Mommy says again.

"Mommy, this is serious!" I kick a pile of leaves and send them flying. "Mommy, why did you and Daddy name me Aviva?"

Before Mommy answers, the big clock on Main Street chimes three times. "Is it three o'clock already?" she asks. "We have to hurry if we're going to make chicken soup for supper."

The minute we get home, Mommy fills a big pot with water and hands me some carrots to wash. "Do you know who taught me to make soup, Emily?"

"Who?" I ask, letting Lulu steal a carrot.

"I learned from my Grandma Ada," says Mommy, chopping celery. "Her chicken soup was so delicious, everyone told her to open a restaurant, but she said, 'Sell my soup? Never! Anyone who is hungry may have a bowl for free.'"

Mommy sets the soup on the stove and then points to my sweater. "Emily, did you lose a button?"

I bring Mommy our sewing box. While she threads a needle, I spill her button collection onto the table. The buttons make a sound like rain.

"Do you know who taught me to sew?" Mommy asks.
I shake my head.

"My Grandma Ada," Mommy says, moving her pin
cushion out of Lulu's reach. "This used to be her
button collection."

I pick out a shiny button shaped like a rose.

"Ada worked in a lace factory," Mommy says, pushing her needle through my sweater. "She was only ten, so at first the boss didn't want to hire her, but as soon as he saw that her stitches were as fine as spider webs, he quickly changed his mind." Mommy ties a knot and snips the thread.

"Emily, what should we do while the soup is cooking?"

"Let's read stories," I say as I run to get some books.
"Did your Grandma Ada teach you to read?"

"Yes she did," Mommy says as I crawl into her lap and Lulu crawls into mine. "Grandma Ada spoke Yiddish as a little girl. She said when she first saw English letters, they looked like little bugs crawling all over the page. She studied the English newspaper every night to learn her ABC's."

"I'm home," Daddy calls. "Do I smell chicken soup?"

"Hi, Daddy!" I race Lulu to the door and throw my arms around him. He scoops me up and carries me to the kitchen. "Did you have a good day, Aviva?"

"My name isn't Aviva," I tell him. "My name is Emily."

"Emily?" Daddy's forehead crinkles.

"Emily," Mommy nods.

After supper Mommy, Daddy, and I work on a jigsaw puzzle together. Then we take Lulu for a walk.

"What a pretty sky," Daddy says, looking up.
"Emily, can you find the Big Dipper?" Mommy
asks.

I tilt my head all the way back.

"There it is," I point. "Mommy, did your
Grandma Ada teach you about the stars?"

"She certainly did," Mommy says. "When Grandma Ada was a girl, she sailed from Russia to America on a great big ship. At night it was cold and dark and scary. But when she saw the same stars in the sky she used to see over her own little village, she knew everything would be all right." Mommy smiles. "Grandma Ada loved the Big Dipper. She said it looked like her soup ladle."

When bedtime comes, Lulu and I climb under the covers. "Goodnight, Emily." Daddy kisses my cheek.

"Sleep tight, Emily." Mommy kisses my other cheek.

"Mommy," I sit up in bed. "Can I ask you something?"

"You just did."

"Can I ask you something else?"

"You just did," Mommy says again, and Daddy chuckles.

"Mommy!" I kick my feet but I'm not really mad. "Mommy, you never told me why you and Daddy named me Aviva."

"I'll tell you," Daddy says, sitting beside me. "When Mommy and I told Grandma Ada we were starting a family, she said, 'That's wonderful! I've waited a hundred years to become a great-grandmother.' But she died before you were born." Mommy looks sad for a minute and Daddy takes her hand.

"In our tradition," Mommy says, "we name our children after someone we loved. Sometimes we choose the same name, sometimes we choose a name that means something like it, and sometimes we choose a name that starts with the same letter. Grandma Ada's Hebrew name was Aviva which means spring—"

"I was born in the spring!" I interrupt Mommy.

"I remember," Mommy laughs. "I was there."

"I was there, too," Daddy says. "And when Mommy and I saw you for the very first time, we knew you would grow up to be as brave and smart and talented and kind as Grandma Ada. So we named you Aviva, in honor of your great-grandmother."

Mommy leans down and kisses my forehead. "Sweet dreams, honey."

Daddy tucks the blanket under my chin. "Sweet dreams, bunny."

I don't say anything.

"Emily?" Daddy whispers. "Are you asleep?"

"My name isn't Emily," I say, snuggling up to Lulu. "My name is Aviva."

## About the Author and Illustrator

**Lesléa Newman** is the author of more than sixty books for readers of all ages including the children's books *Matzo Ball Moon*, *A Sweet Passover*, *Runaway Dreidel!* and *Here is the World: A Year of Jewish Holidays*. Her literary awards include poetry fellowships from the National Endowment for the Arts and the Massachusetts Artists Foundation, an American Library Association Honor, and a Sydney Taylor Honor. She is a former poet laureate of Northampton, MA, and lives in Holyoke, MA.

**Ag Jatkowska** was born in Gdansk, Poland and grew up by the cold Baltic Sea. She graduated from the Academy of Fine Arts in Gdansk with an M.A. in Graphic Design and Illustration. She lives in Bath, England.